Shallbelove

by John Fulton

To Sharna

Shallbelove

Far, far, far away is the star called Shallbelove. If you never heard of this star, don't be surprised. Most people don't know the star. It is a small star, and its beautiful glow is seen only by a few. And most of those who see it live in the land of Murh.

Shallbelove was made with love and care by The Old Starmaker. At night the beauty of the little star would shine through millions of miles and give joy to the people who live in the land of Murh.

But the star Shallbelove did not know this. He only knew how alone he felt, how tired he was, how sad his heart. And he grew more sad and more tired, and the light from his star began to dim and dim. And his heart—for stars have hearts as humans do—grew heavy.

Of course, The Old Starkeeper carried his X-30Z Alarm Detector with him everywhere he went, all through the universe. (For the job of keeping the universe in tune and balance was a very difficult thing to do. So he needed the most modern tools and a no-nonsense approach to his demanding job.)

In the last thousand years or so The Old Starkeeper had been noticing how the star Shallbelove was flickering. It was not as strong as it had been when he, The Old Starkeeper, made Shallbelove long, long ago.

But The Old Starkeeper was busy. You know how busy you are just to keep your room cleaned up. Think of it like this. The Old Starkeeper had to keep a gazillion rooms cleaned up. Whew! He had a lot on his mind, a star here, a comet there, a moon way down yonder.

Go outside some night and look at all the lights in the sky. The Old Starkeeper had to tune them and tweak them and keep them moving and balanced, and, whew! you can just imagine how busy he was.

But he could not overlook Shallbelove much longer. Shallbelove was not only a sick and failing star. It also was the star that The Old Starkeeper loved the best. He had made it last of all the stars, and he had worked hard to make it the most perfect and beautiful star of all.

And he had worked and worked, and then even he had marveled at the wonder of his work. And then he had rested…and he had not rested since.

And there was another reason--an even bigger reason--for The Old Starkeeper's concern.

Shallbelove was the balance of the universe. If Shallbelove should fail to hold up its end, the whole universe would be thrown out of whack. Consequences would he dire. The cleanup of the wreckage would take The Old Starkeeper eons, simply eons, lots and lots of years to fix. That's for sure.

And so he hurried to Shallbelove to have a heart-to-heart talk with Shallbelove.

"Shallbelove, I see you are failing, but even failing your beauty, ah, how sweet you glow, how soft you are, a star to call home almost," and The Old Starkeeper sighed.

"Old Starkeeper, what a delightful surprise! How wonderful to see you. But how tired you look. Here, sit. Sit and rest."

"It has been so long, dear Old Starkeeper. You are the only one in eons who has come here and who has touched me and let me give a little of myself. It is just great to see you."

"Ah," satisfied-sighed The Old Starkeeper, for Shallbelove was a wondrous star, a wonderful place to be.

But, then remembering why he was here, The Old Starkeeper pulled himself up to a kind of attention. "You may not be so glad when I tell you why I came. You are ill, Shallbelove. Don't try to deny it. My X-30Z Alarm Detector…"

The Old Starkeeper did a double-take, for the light which had been so red so long now was glowing green for good.

He gave the device a whack to make it adjust, but the X-30Z continued glowing green.

"Hmmm," The Old Starkeeper said, "This is strange. This has been showing you increasingly sick—very sick, but now shows you healthy, alert and well. What the dangnabbletoes is wrong with this thing?"

"I have been worried." The Old Starkeeper looked straight at Shallbelove. "Very, very worried. You are the star which balances the universe, you know. Plus, of course, I have been worried about you—yourself."

"Yes, yes," said Shallbelove, "I understand all that, but you can imagine how lonely it is here, no one to talk to. I am so far, far away, so remote. It is--I don't know quite how to say it--it is not the same as when you came here," and now Shallbelove looked straight at The Old Starkeeper, "such a long, long time ago."

2

"Even though you look tired, it is wonderful to see you," Shallbelove said. "You should not worry so. Seeing you, having you here, I'm feeling better. I feel fine. You shouldn't worry so."

"Not worry? Dangnabbletoes," The Old Starkeeper said with a sudden burst, "here you are failing--failing, failing, failing…my finest work, a robust, beautiful star hanging in the balance. But in this workaday universe, I can't think about that much. I've got to make the whole thing hold together. I don't suppose that makes sense to you. Oh, why should it? How could you know my problems? No one else does."

"Tell me then," said Shallbelove.

"Tell you? Oh, what good is there in that? The universe is in awful shape and getting worse every dangnabbletoes second. You are sad and lonely to the point that I may have to retire you to the old star graveyard and put in a more functional star in your place. If you only knew what the Princess Marisa thinks of you, you might feel a lot better. I haven't sat down and talked like this since the last time I was here. I really should be getting on with my work. Time's wasting."

"What? Tell me about Marisa. You say she is a princess."

"Oh, what's the use in telling you all that? It will only make you sad. These last few hours should be as happy for you as we can make them."

"Tell me!" said Shallbelove in such a way that made The Old Starkeeper sit back sharply.

"All right, I'll tell you, but it's not a very pretty story. The land of Murh is nearer to us than any other planet. It is the home of the Barnswartians, who live in the dark and ravelly forest. They eat bugs and worms. They are an ugly sort, mean and warlike. That would be all except for one thing," The Old Starkeeper fought back a yawn.

"What is that?" said Shallbelove, intent and pressing.

"What…What is what," the Old Starkeeper said, yawning again, his eyes blinking back sleep.

"What is so bad about the Barnswartians?. . .except for what thing?"

"Oh, Princess Marisa and her father, King Goodlord, and their people. They fear for their lives. You know if I could ever get this universe straightened around, I could spend a little more time putting the right things in the right place.

"Like you, Shallbelove, you're right. I did promise you to drop by more often than I have. But, dangnabbletoes, I get so blamed busy. Well, it doesn't matter now."

"And why is that?" said Shallbelove, again in a tone expecting an answer.

The Old Starkeeper crooked his eye. "Because...well, Shallbelove it doesn't—some things, some little nice things—don't matter so much when you just have to do what you have to do."

"It doesn't matter that you are my finest star. It doesn't matter how much I hate to have to replace you with a star that may not be so pretty, but keeps its balance and gets the job done."

"It doesn't matter that Marisa looks to you each night for hope. It doesn't matter how lonely you are. Everywhere I go in the universe I see the same things, see the same problems."

"Most of the time, I manage to put my own feelings aside and just do my job. That's what it's all about anyway."

Again The Old Starkeeper stifled a yawn, this time a bigger one than before.

"Where is the land of Murh?" said Shallbelove, so softly that The Old Starkeeper barely heard.

"You have the most musical voice in the universe," The Old Starkeeper said. "It is a beautiful voice to hear, soothing and quiet. It puts my heart at ease. It makes me want to rest."

"Where is Murh?" said Shallbelove again, this time softer even than before.

"It is a long, long way from here but straight out that way," he said pointing toward a great void in space. If you look close you can see it deep and dark away in space."

"How long by Starbright passage?" Shallbelove asked.

"Hey, you mustn't think of that. That would do us all in. You are barely strong enough to keep your end up as it is. The Old Starkeeper looked down at his alarm box. "Well, I see you're not quite in the danger zone, but you don't have enough strength to send your Starbright there."

"I'm all right. I feel fine. In fact, I have never felt better."

"Well, I wish I could say the same. Listen, I can't sit here talking to you this way. I have work to do."

"Sit back a moment. Listen, I will play you soft music. Sit back and close your eyes and try not to carry on for a while about all these things you worry about. Everyone needs a little time to rest.

"Of course, you can get too much of that too," Shallbelove said in a pointed way and looked with meaning at The Old Starkeeper, who in self defense shut his eyes and leaned back to rest.

And before he knew it, The Old Starkeeper, despite himself, fell fast asleep.

And almost at once, Shallbelove sent his Starbright streaking off toward the Land of Murh.

A Starbright is a special thing that stars have. It is a light reflected from a sun or generated from within the star. Usually you see it as a beam of light far distant in the sky, but it also can he sent in a twinkling to any place the heart of the star wishes to send it. And in that place, the light can live and dance and shine and make the hearts of those who see it shine. It can point the way to safety, or dance to make heavy hearts light. It can make itself known through the love it feels and makes others feel.

But Starbright is rare because it takes so much of the star's energy to keep the Starbright going. Had he not drifted off into a deep sleep, The Old Starkeeper would have been sorely—sorely—troubled to know what Shallbelove was up to.

And so it was that the Starbright from Shallbelove whisked off to the land of Murh.

At first Starbright did not see the young girl. The forest was deep and dark, and the growing things seemed to move close around them. The growing things felt like they had thousands of hairs. They were wet and moving, undulating, and the place was swarmy with bugs.

In the dim light, Starbright could make out a marshy swamp. But the whole place was cast in shadows. He could see nothing clearly.

Then he heard a whimper. It came from a young girl crying. She was trudging through the marshy waters up to her knees. Her face was streaked with tears and dirt. Her clothes were wet and matted. She moved slowly through the waters with a kind of swimming motion. She had a desperate look in her eyes. She held something high, near her chin clutched tightly with both hands. She moved with determination toward a place the Starbright could not see.

At first she did not see Shallbelove's Starbright, so focused was she on the place she wanted to reach.

When she finally did see him, she moved with a start, almost dropping what she carried.

But she quickly righted herself and looked with young-old wise eyes at the strange new light. Starbright did a little dance of light to show her there was no reason for fear. Starbright moved left and right and up and down and around in circles.

Finally, slowly she smiled. "Who are you?" she said.

Starbright started dancing again. And again she smiled….until a sound thrashing through the swamp behind them sent her smile away and left in its place a great look of fear.

She smoothed down her hair with one quick hand. With her other hand, she clutched the thing she carried more tightly than ever. The sound grew louder.

The girl showed more fear and lunged off through the swamp away from the thrashing noise.

The sounds grew louder. Shallbelove's Starbright moved this way and that, not knowing what to do.   Then into the dim light came dark and ugly men—or at least what Shallbelove understood from The Old Starkeeper to be men.

Or were they animals, Starbright wondered? Their bodies were thick with muscles and even in the dimness shimmered with the water from the swamp. Hair grew everywhere on their bodies, in a great scraggly mass upon their heads. There were three of them, carrying clubs and spears. One of them, the tallest, youngest and best looking of them, carried a shield and wore a kind of helmet. There was something else about him that the Starbright felt at once. But what the something was he could not say.

"That way," the young one said, pointing with a sword in a direction away from Starbright (who had taken to hiding as best he could behind a slimy vine).

And off they all slushed through the hot, dank swamp which gave off foul odors as they jostled the air about.

Starbright waited as they crashed away through the swamp. Breaking out of a kind of trance, Starbright suddenly remembered the girl and set off in the direction she had gone.

He caught up with the girl just as she was disappearing into a strange, small hole where the undergrowth had been chopped away. Starbright watched her disappear into the hole and he followed after her. As he moved through the hole, he saw it led into a tunnel, not really a tunnel, but a little passage cut through the thick undergrowth. In passing through it, he saw the vines clutch at her. They seemed already to be growing back around them.

Then just as suddenly they came into sunlight.

The girl crawled through the hole and went into a small, open clearing. The sunlight was startling, a welcome warmth from the dank and empty cold of the swamp. She put down her burden, which the Starbright now saw to be a pail full of fruits and nuts. She brushed at her clothes to knock away most of the grime as well as some ugly looking bugs which went scurrying away into the swamp.

"My dear, my dear," said an old man the Starbright had not noticed, "I see you have come safely back to us again with fruit. Ah my darling, Marisa, we have been so worried. Each time our concern grows greater."

He was a large man, and his voice was strong though it trembled as he spoke. He stood as he spoke, but stood uncertainly. The girl picked up the pail of food and went to him, and setting down the fruit, invited him to sit down and eased him into a natural chair made from leaves and grass in the clearing.

"My dear, Marisa, I fear for us, my lovely daughter. I should be strong and keep my fears hidden from you. But you must see how each day the light is a little less bright. The swampy forest encroaches, The last of our followers are weak with hunger. I fear they shall put their fate in the hands of Gufalgar. Ah," sighed the old man, more heavily, more sadly even than had The Old Starkeeper.

"How can my uncle Gufalgar be so mean, papa?"

"Revenge, my dear. And power. He wants power. He was not content with all the land south of Hecuba Sea. He wants all of Murh," The old man's voice trailed off, "and it seems he shall have it this week or the next. It is only a matter of time until the swarmy forest blots out our sun. They will discover our passage to find the exotic fruit. Then they will come for us, and who knows what will happen."

"We must keep our hope, father. Perhaps Rogan…"

"Ah," said the old man with sudden fire, "do not speak to me of that young blackguard. Without him, Gufalgar could not so easily have had his way. For all his physical strength, Rogan is weak, for he does not know his own heart. Rogan! I know of your childish feelings for him. You should forget them. He is a work of evil. He is bad."

The girl did not answer directly. "Still, father, we must hope. Food will keep us alive. To really be alive, we must keep alive the food of hope as well. Here, let us eat the food I brought," and so they did.

The sun departed and they lit a small candle. "Even the candles are about all gone," the old man said. "When there is no light they will come sneaking out of the swamp and take us or devour us or some awful such thing. Ah, Marisa, I wish I were stronger. I wish we could do something."

"Well, father," said the girl, tucking him firmly beneath covers in the rugged little bed of straw, "we must hope."

"Ah, ah," was all he said to that, the sound of a dying soul.

After putting her father to bed, Marisa strolled out into the open area and looked up to the heavens..

Looking up as well, much to his surprise, Starbright saw only one star in the sky--a dim star, flickering, and far, far away. "Why, that is me. That is the star Shallbelove," Starbright said to himself.

"Hello, my little star," said the girl, Marisa. And the Starbright immediately remembered that The Old Starkeeper had mentioned a girl Marisa who talked to her star every night. What a small universe, Starbright thought to himself.

"There that's better. You brighten before my very eyes. I wonder why that is. Whatever it is, it is wonderful. But not, I'm afraid, wonderful enough." And she too sighed.

"Each day I go for food, I am more frightened than the last time. And father is right, the forest is growing in around us. Soon we too will be taken darkly into the swampy forest. That's all that saves us, the light we use to protect ourselves. When that is gone they will come and take us."

"Gufalgar will have the whole land of Murh. I hope he will be happy then, for no one else will be, not even those who serve him. They only do it out of fear...Oh, Rogan, I know your loyalty to your own father, but what of your love for me? Is it all gone? Do you really believe that being a Prince of Darkness is more than the love we have for one another. Can't you remember the sunlight and the meadows where we used to walk? My dear, dear Rogan. Starbright, I wish I knew your name."

The Starbright was speechless, but he kept thinking, "Shallbelove, Shallbelove, Shallbelove."

"Yes, I know it comes to me," Marisa said. "I'll call you Shallbelove."

"Yes, that's right." Starbright did a little light leap of pleasure.

"You are like the forest though, little star, Shallbelove. You seem so dear and yet each night more dim, more far away. I wonder why tonight you seem somehow so close. Oh, there it is again," the girl exclaimed for she had caught sight of Starbright hiding partly behind a vine.

"Come here," she said in her musical voice, and out shyly from behind the vine Starbright came.

"I was so afraid the first time I saw you because of those awful men who are always searching and that awful place. It is creepy, don't you think?"

Starbright did a trick The Old Starkeeper had taught him, moving up and down in the air, like a person shaking his head yes.

"I'm not afraid of you now. I can see you are a friendly little light. Were you sent here to protect me?" Again Starbright moved up and down lightly. "I wonder how you can?"

"I can only hope there is someone or something that can save us, but I'm afraid father is right. Soon the forest will close over this sunlit glen and the few who are with us will give up. I don't blame them for they must try to live also. But the once great land of Murh shall all be one dark swamp. Soon there shall be no light at all like yours, my light-dancing little friend. Without light there shall be no love--a great price to pay for the power Gufalgar craves."

She sighed a final time and then went back to the little bower. She went to bed by the flickering light of the candle.

Starbright first sensed only the forbidding quiet, but then he felt a kind of movement. The forest, he saw, was moving. Its dark twiny branches and wet gnarled tree trunks were moving in around them, ever so slowly so as hardly to be seen.

But the movement, forbidding as it was, was so slow Starbright could see the good king and the beautiful young princess would be safe from the forest, at least through the night.

Starbright decided to go off through the forest and see what he might see this time of night in the dark heart of the dark forest. He went looking for the tunnel through the vines and saw it had grown smaller since he passed through it a short time before.

He went through the tunnel with only his light to guide him. His way was fairly easy for the vines seemed to shrink back away from his Starbright.

Everywhere he went he saw wet vines grow thicker and more dense. He felt the cold wetness all around him, chilling his light and making him remember how weak his light had become. Still he moved on through the darkness, lured by the promise of learning the answer to a mystery.

He heard voices. They were mumbled and hushed, and he could not make out what the voices said. He moved toward the voices, slowly, slowly. In a kind of opening in the forest, he could make out dim shapes. His own light could have made them more clear, but he wanted to get as close as possible to see what was going on. It was hard to tell. Starbright could barely make out the dark shapes dressed in ragged, dirty clothes. The shapes seemed to move in the swamp as if they were bathing. Only they were putting mud and slimy vines all over their bodies. They were laughing like crazy.

"It will be very soon," said one of the largest figures in the center of the swamp. "Soon their candles will be gone, and the forest will grow in around them and then, when there is no light, we shall attack and capture the king and that so precious Marisa!"

And the one who spoke then fell into a cackling, hideous laugh, and the others around him took up his awful laugh like a cackling chorus.

Then Starbright heard something else—the sound of heavy chains. He could just make out the stooped shoulders and dark-weary faces of men and women and even children who were not enjoying the mud bath.

These must be the ones, thought Starbright, who have given up to the evil Gufalgar, living as prisoners, stripped of pride.

The sight made Starbright so angry that he forgot where he was, showed himself and was startled by the reaction.

"Aaargh," yelled the big man throwing his arms in front of his eyes. "What is that light, put it out, put it out. Kill the light. Quick. Kill that light."

And out of the mud bath rushed several Barnswartians, swinging huge clubs and swords. Starbright dodged and weaved, but the Barnswartians kept clubbing and stabbing at him until he decided to retreat back through the forest, back the way he had come.

He moved fast out of there and after a while the sounds chasing him died away and he realized how tired he was. He sat down at the base of a tree to rest. So you can imagine how surprised he was to hear another voice, a man's voice, but more pleasant than any Barnswartian. It seemed to come from just the other side of the tree.

"I wish there was someone to talk to. Someone who could hear my words and speak to me, someone who might understand a little and make this awful lonely feeling go away, if only for a little while."

"I'll talk to you," said Starbright, peeking around the tree and surprising the man who was as grim and dirty as the others he had seen, but whose face was fine-boned. The man's eyes were troubled, but Starbright could see at once that they meant him no harm.

"No, do not be afraid," Starbright said. "I would not harm you even if I could. I know how it is to feel lonely. You see I am that star you see on nights like this. I am far away from everything, everyone. I get awfully lonely."

"You are that star? Why that must be Marisa's star. You are that star? My gosh. You're…like real."

"Oh yes, there are many marvels in the universe. I have learned, that in a different form, the real form of myself, I am that star that young Marisa watches and marvels at. My gosh, right back to you."

"I am that star Shallbelove. And here I am the Starbright of the Star Shallbelove. It's pretty complicated." Starbright went on to tell the young, strong man how he had come to the Land of Murh.

"I must be going back to the Star Shallbelove very soon. I suppose The Old Starkeeper will retire me. Then I'm afraid Marisa will have no star to marvel at, to dream upon."

"No," the young man said. "The dank forest will cover all the rest of Murh in no time flat. Then all the land will turn to swamp. My father will be king, and Marisa will be our prisoner." He said all this without joy. "Ah, ah, my beautiful Marisa, what shall happen to you then?"

"She will be a prisoner like those others back there then?"

"Yes, just so."

"But why don't you help her? You seem to care about her."

"Marisa, my dearest. We used to walk the hills and pick flowers together when there were flowers in Murh. I made her a swing on the limb of a great tree.

"We used to go there and swing and talk and run. Marisa would put flowers in her hair. It makes me sad to think how happy we were, how much we laughed."

"My gosh, you must be Rogan. I sensed how lonely she must have felt when she spoke of you. I'd say she loves you."

"And here I am."

"Then why don't you go to her and help her against the Barnswartians? I don't know, but you don't seem their type."

"Don't say that! I am of their blood. I am the oldest son of King Gufalgar. I must follow my father's rules. I must honor my father and do as he says. That is our custom. It may be wrong--and oh, it seems so--but that is what I must do. I must even lead Barnswartian troops. It is I who must capture King Goodlord and the Princess Marisa and bring them to my father. There is no way out of it. I am tormented to death."

Starbright listened quietly and the silence fell in around them except for the soft lapping of the swamp against their little island.

Finally he spoke. "Well, I don't know. I have never been a living, breathing man, but those feelings are pretty much the same here and on Shallbelove and everywhere. Stars have feelings. I have feelings. I have feelings for loving and loneliness and even feelings of loyalty for The Old Starkeeper. I have fondness and a feeling of loyalty to him. I am grateful to him, of course."

"Without him, I couldn't he here or anywhere else for that matter, but that only goes so far. He left me alone for millions of years. You can't really imagine how lonely it is to be a star and not know if anyone cares for you. He told me I would probably perish if I made this trip. He said I would use up all my energy and that I would cause him more work than he had had in centuries."

"Well, that was all very fine for him, but what did I have to lose? I had nothing to live for. He needed a rest, and I lulled him to sleep and shot straightaway here to see about the trouble he said you were having here in Murh. I suppose that's disloyal, and you can judge that for yourself. But I can tell you this. I will never be lonely in quite the way I was before. I have been kissed by Marisa, and talked to you, even if you are her enemy."

"Oh, don't say that. I am not her enemy."

"But you are the one who will capture her and take her in chains to the dank forest. I don't see how that makes you her friend!"

"Ah, don't talk any longer. I don't want to hear any more."

"Well, I want to talk!" Starbright said with sudden self assertion. "I have been twinkling forever and ever for no real reason. Now I have someone who understands, and I will be heard, and if I had ever picked flowers with that fine young girl and built her a swing to swing in the great tree in the meadow by the stream, I wouldn't be sulking here and make it sound all right that I am going to capture her and chain her and maybe kill her after all."

"You. I'll tell you who I'll kill. I'll kill you," said Rogan with a sudden fierceness, screaming the words. He sounded like a wild animal. With one great swing of his sword, the tree, five feet in diameter, went crashing down, but just in time the Starbright jumped aside. The swinging sword missed him.

As Starbright streaked for the tunnel to escape and hide he looked back in surprise to see that Rogan was not pursing him, but sat now with his head buried in his huge hands. Rogan was weeping with great huge gasps for air.

When Starbright finally emerged through the light at the end of the tunnel, dawn was breaking, wrapped in sunlight. Times were mixed up. Starbright realized how tired he was, barely yawned and fell asleep.

He didn't know how long he slept, or even why he woke. There she was, Marisa. Starbright lay with his head in her lap. "I was worried about little Starbright. I thought your light had gone. You looked so old and gray. Your light, it flickers low."

"I do feel tired, more tired than ever before, I really should get back to Shallbelove. I hope I have enough energy left to make the journey home. I wish I could have been more help and comfort to you, Marisa."

"It is always a great honor to meet a star, especially the star I have wished upon ever since I was a little girl."

"And I can't tell you how wonderful it has been to know a real live princess."

Now almost fully awake, despite his tiredness, Starbright saw how dark it had become around them so quickly. "It is night, just like that, again," he exclaimed.

"No, but I wish it were. It is the forest. As you have been sleeping, the last of our candles burned out. The forest has grown around us. Soon I fear the Barnswartians will come for us, and Gufalgar shall become king of the land."

"I can't understand his cruelty at all," Starbright said.

"I suppose it started when Gufalgar tried to win my mother. Instead she married my father, because of his kindness and gentleness. Gufalgar never forgot, never forgave, according to what my father told me. Gufalgar hated so much that he developed a rare disease. In his passion and hate he became allergic to light. With his followers, he tried to overthrow my father as king, but succeeded only in killing the queen, the woman he had loved. My mother. This made him all the more twisted and hateful. Forced by the light, he escaped back into the forest. We all thought Gufalgar had gone to the forest to die. We even held a solemn funeral for him, but the forest gave him comfort and brought him back to health—if you can call it that. Word came back from time to time that he was alive and living, living well--off the bugs and dank plants of the forest."

"At first we were sorry for him. Our people were sorry for him, but then came his threats that he would conquer the land of Murh. Some of our people laughed. My father warned us we should not laugh at Gufalgar. He was so sad and vile there was no laughter in him."

"After a while, some of our people began to disappear. Mainly they were the people who made all the crops grow. Gufalgar put them to work and used them to grow the forest. The forest became larger and darker. No one of our people is safe. The risk is to be captured or killed. So that is the way it is for us in Murh. Our days are numbered."

"I'm glad you are awake now for you must hurry on your journey back to your star. Remember you need to keep the balance of the universe. If you should fail to do that, you will have failed at everything little Starbright."

"To fail at holding up the universe makes me less sad than failing the love you felt for me."

"No, you did not fail. Love is always special. Love has a way of living forever. I don't know quite how, but love is not just something that stops. Hurry. They are coming. You must fly away while you can still find your way through the forest, through the tops of the trees."

Reluctantly Starbright moved slowly out of Marisa's grasp and rose higher and higher, through the grasping limbs of the trees. There was a heavy cover of cloud above the trees, and rain was falling hard--so hard it made the light of the Starbright, still weak from wandering, nearly sputter and go out.

But then Starbright was startled to life by the sound of a huge army suddenly come crashing through the forest,

"Aarrgh," Starbright heard the unmistakable voice of Gufalgar. Though Starbright could not see, he could easily imagine a host of Barnswartians crashing in upon the few helpless survivors. Oh, what could he do for Marisa and her father, the good King Goodlord.

In his agony and doubt, Starbright looked toward home, toward Shallbelove, the distant star—where it would have been if he could have seen through the dark and ominous clouds.

Then, following his heart so that it almost burst, he decided for Marisa who had loved him first in all these millions years.

He decided. Starbright would make his most brilliant light. Then maybe, just maybe, it would clear away the clouds and rain and so scorch the dark, dank trees and vines that they would shrink back.

And so, putting all his drained and tired energy into it, he glowed. He tried to glow.

He glowed and yet there seemed so little light. His heart seemed fit to burst, and so Starbright tried to glow brighter, aching, all muscles straining. Weak and dizzy, so little energy and he tried to glow brighter. And the clouds parted. The rain stopped. The grasping, swaying dark branches paused in their grasping and shrank back.

Still Starbright could not see what was happening in the dark forest down below. And so with all the energy he had left, Starbright tried to glow still more.

This time the limbs snapped back. The vines slithered away. The forest opened like a great wide meadow. So burning hot was the glow from Shallbelove's Starbright that the Barnswartians who had lived for years in the dank, dark forest cast off their shields and threw down their clubs.

They grasped at their clothes and tried to shield their eyes from Starbright's terrible light. Starbright saw one more clearly than the others. He was dirtier than nearly all the Barnswartians and larger than most of them, His skin was lizard white, indescribably pale. He was trying vainly to get back to the forest. Unlike the others, whose eyes were like slits, he was bug-eyed, but unseeing. He was trying to escape the light, but slipping and falling, using his once deadly sword as a walking cane to hurry himself along. Right in his path was the Princess Marisa.

He didn't seem to see her, but sensed that Marisa was there.

"Aarrrgh, came the unmistakable guttural scream of Gufalgar. "Marisa, it is you, who will taste now the sword of Barnswartia." Gufalgar raised the sword high, blind and evil and ready to strike her down.

Starbright, exhausted, could not generate another extra ounce of light. Starbright's heart went sinking. Gufalgar's sword raised up. Gufalgar was consumed in the power of hate as Starbright's had been in love.

But as the great sword came crashing down--out of nowhere came Rogan. He took the blow from his father's sword on his own sword and shield so that Gufalgar's sword was shattered into pieces. Gufalgar's shield was smashed away.

Rogan put down his sword and looked at his bloodied arm which had taken Gufalgar's blow. Stunned and in shock, Rogan just stood there.

"Rogan," screamed the insane Gufalgar. "You turned against me. You turned against your father. Arrghh."

Gufalgar, still strong with hate, reached out, taking Rogan's sword and raising it high again as if to strike Rogan dead, this time to bring the sword down upon his oldest son's head.

Still not quite seeing, his arm broken and bloody, Rogan looked upon his father with stricken eyes. Perhaps in the dim vision he had left, Gufalgar may have really looked at his oldest son for the first time in many years. Perhaps--for he seemed to pause for a split second. In that briefest of moments, Rogan, no longer wispy and unsure, took his dagger from his belt and thrust it into his father's heart.

"Aarrghh," screamed Gufalgar, dying.

And the other Barnswartians, pale and struggling toward the safety of the forest, seeing the death of their evil king, had all the fight slip out of them. The last few of them, who still carried their swords and shields, threw them down or tried to use their shields against the bright sun that broke through the clouds above.

"Father, father." said Rogan, bending over the hulk of his father, the dead king Gufalgar. "Can you forgive me? Can I ever be forgiven?"

Marisa went to him and put her arms around the fine young man dressed in filthy rags. She held him close and cooed to him gently as he wept. "It was not you, Rogan, but your father who first raised his fist in anger. If you had not killed him he would have killed you. You acted to protect yourself—to protect all of us. He would not have tried to kill you if you had not tried to save me. What then? Are you so much

16

in pain of heart that you have saved my life?"

"Oh, no, Marisa, never that. But my father lies dead there."

"Yes, but look around you. You will see the armies of hate and war have laid down their swords and shields. Now there will be peace in our land, and oh, Rogan, I missed you so. I love you so."

With that the great hulking sobbing hero took the frail girl in his arms. Time seemed to stand still for them, lost as they were in their world apart. At first they did not understand what the gathering people were cheering as with one voice. "Long live the prince! Long live the princess!"

But time could not stand still for Starbright. With renewed energy, still dancing above the tree tops to keep from plummeting back to earth, he saw the work of love begin to open a great green valley to push the forest back. Starbright smiled to himself with joy and pride at the happy scene below. "I did my job here," he said quietly, but remembered at once the other big job in keeping the universe together. He looked once more back at the people of Murh.

Men and women and children of Murh were now gathering around Marisa and Rogan. Starbright sensed they already were planning a great party to mark the great wedding soon to come.

Then fixing sight on the distant star Shallbelove and gathering what energy he had left, Starbright shot himself homeward with the last ounces of his strength, hoping it would be enough.

Or what he thought would be the last ounces of his strength. But when the Starbright returned and again became part of Shallbelove, he felt stronger than before—stronger than for a long, long time before.

He was also surprised to find The Old Starkeeper still fast asleep.

"Wake up, wake up, you sleepy thing," said Shallbelove in a voice not at all in the manner of his usual voice.

"Wha...huh," said The Old Starkeeper, coming partly awake blinking his eyes open and shut and making a monstrous yawn. " Oh, yes, as I was saying. So you see, Shallbelove, it's absolutely impossible for you to go off to that planet. I'd like to help you out but I've got the universe to think of after all...and it's absolutely out of the question."

"Oh shut up and eat ambrosia and drink nectar. There are things I want to tell you."

"Can't do that. I've got to attend to keeping the old universe humming, don't you know?"

"Yes, yes, I know all about that and more. I 'm beginning to think I know more than you do. You go around busy-busy minding things and moving things around. And maybe you have lost sight of what is really important. I'm talking about love and kindness and doing something because it's important to you, and resting and enjoying yourself once in a while.

"Well, dangnabbletoes," harrumphed The Old Starkeeper, "that's all very well and good, but, after all, remember your own failing strength and energy put everything off kilter. There's the whole universe to think about. I can't spend all my time with one little star. I've got a serious problem—how to keep a universal balance after your light fails.

"Listen, Mr. Old Starkeeper, I have never felt better. Here. Test my energy on that stupid machine of yours."

And The Old Starkeeper did. "Well, well, well. That's very strange indeed. You've got a rating in the Thirty ZH 10th Megazone! Top flight, none brighter. That simply cannot be. Let me see again." And so he did, and the reading came the same again.

"Dangnabbletoes, you're pulling a trick on me, Shallbelove, and with the whole universe at stake I don't appreciate that very much."

"The only trick I'm pulling on you, Old Starkeeper, is the trick of love. I have loved and now I burn and glow with fires deep inside me, deeper than even you can see. Your fine universe is not hanging in the balance because of me, the mighty Shallbelove. Your immediate troubles are over. There is no crisis."

"I just don't know…" The Old Starkeeper said, stretching his arms and legs.

"You sleep on it," said Shallbelove, "pleasant dreams."

…And in his dreaming, The Old Starkeeper saw how Shallbelove had sent his Starbright to the Land of Murh and how Starbright had brought peace and love.

And across the miles of space, far, far, far away glowed Shallbelove.

Rogan and Marisa stood gazing at the sky, smiling in joy and love at the bright star they saw--so much brighter than all the other stars as to be a new star, their star of love.

"Shalbelove" was inspired by two events-- the birth of our older daughter, Sharna, and musings on a starry night a short while later, That "short while later" was more than 50 years ago. I have been writing and rewriting "Shallbelove" pretty much, off and on, ever since. So this "almost-qualifies-as-a-life-work" is as good as its going to get. In that spirit--Voila! Telling of love and hope, which I hope the story conveys, is, I think, a story that cannot be told too often.

I, John Fulton, am proud to have found, wooed and been married to Darlene all these years. I am proud of our daughters, Sharna and Tamra, no longer my little girls--now grown, productive, smart, and--in my unbiased opinion--really good people. I am proud to be a graduate of the University of Texas, Austin. Hook 'em Horns! My adopted state of Colorado has been good to me. Came to the Denver area in 1959, been here, except for one year ever since. Sheri Smith, who took this photo on her cellphone, is my long time buddy. Patricia Noonan, another great friend, did the artwork for the story with graciousness and seeming ease. Pat saw what I wanted when I wasn't really sure what I wanted. I think they captured the images.

John Fulton
Aurora, Colorado
January 2018